Yesterday I Found an A

Written by Maggie Blossom

Illustrated by J.T. Winik and Lauren Pashuk

Yesterday I was home alone,
Just me and my friend the mouse.
When **SUDDENLY** I heard a noise,
And went looking around the house.

I went to the room next door
And opened it wide.
I wanted to see
What was hiding inside.

"Are you scared?" called the mouse.

"Not at all," I lied.

I could not stop shaking,
No matter how hard I tried.

That is when yesterday I found an **A**! It was hiding in the very next room.
And out rolled some apples, an accordion, and an airplane went zipping by...ZOOM!
And then I got nervous, afraid things may go wrong.
Because the rest of the alphabet? Well, they had all come along.

And the **B** brought some butterflies, a bee, and a bear.
And a **BILLION** balloons burst out into the air.

The C came with a cat, and a clock, and a clown.
And we formed a parade, and they gave me a crown.

The D delivered a daisy, which is always good luck.
But he also brought along a drum-drumming duck.

And who held the daisy? Why, an elephant you see,
Who said she was there as a guest of the E.
But the E also brought along eight excited eggs.
And they flittered all about the poor elephant's legs.

It was an awesome surprise to find all that next door,
And to also discover footprints on the floor.
So I followed the footprints to see the *next* room next door.
After seeing A to E...something told me there was more...

And when the footprints from **F** finally came to an end,
I discovered a frog, four fish, and my friend!

"FRED?" I asked. "What are **you** doing here?"
"HE'S NOT ALONE!" shouted the frog. "Follow me this way, my dear."

And what did we find in the *next,* next room door?
Why G had a golden goose gliding all over the floor.

My friend mouse was with **H**, high atop a hobby horse,
Followed by a hat, who was hopping, of course!

Letter I had invited an inchworm too big to hide in a rug,
And an ice cream cone so huge that Fred gave it a hug!

J jumped for joy when Jack-in-the-Box came,
And a JILLION jellybeans just joined in the game.

Then **K** and a kangaroo came by, and her kid dropped a key.

And L brought a lollipop-licking lion who would not share with me.

But I didn't mind because **M** made my day,
By bringing a monkey with music to play,
Who gave me a mustache, which looked marvelous, I say.
Then me, the monkey, and the mouse all marched away.

Fred and letter N did not march along.
Fred was too busy counting the nine notes in our song.

O and an octopus both came in at one time.
The octopus was writing an oranges rhyme.
The octopus had also just started juggling.
He had been rhyming quite well, but now he was struggling.

"This is hard," said the octopus. "Nothing rhymes with orange..."

We left the octopus to ponder. We had so much to see.
We turned to the door and yelled, "WHAT YA GOT, P ?"

Then the P came in parading the prettiest pig we had seen,

Followed quite closely by a Q and a queen.

The queen needed her **R** since it brought her red rug,
And her robot that straightened things out with a tug.

S sauntered in with a snake six feet tall,
And a smiling, swinging soldier who caused me to fall.

T trotted in with twin dolls, Myrtle and Gertel,
Who were marching in time with a cute patchwork turtle.

Then U brought in something green and ugly with a frown,
Flying up in an umbrella that had swung upside down.

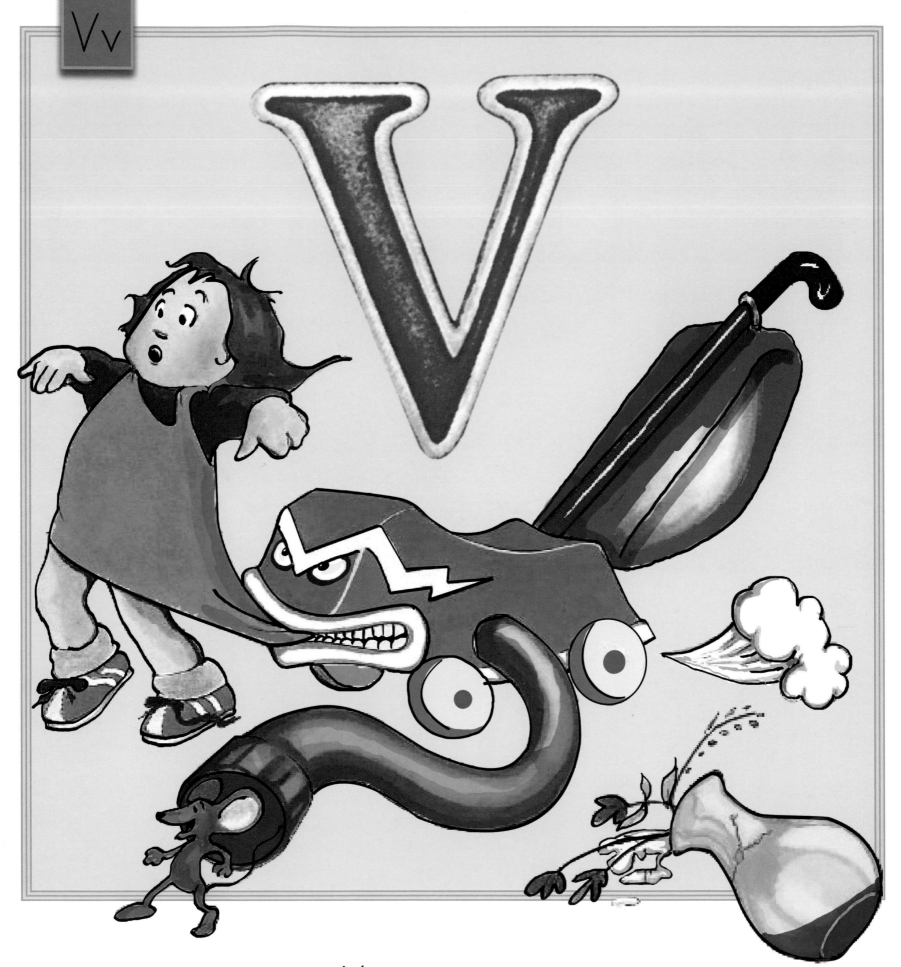

VRRROOOOM went the vacuum as it gave V a chase,
And snagged onto my dress and then knocked down a vase.

Then W walked in and things got really wild.
There was a water-spouting whale in a wagon! Fred just smiled.
"WHOA, Fred, what is going on here?" I said.
"Mmmmmmmm, this watermelon is delicious," said Fred.

Now you may start to wonder if this story is all true.
But X brought an X-ray so you can see through,
All the way to my bones—I have nothing to hide.
You can even ask the mouse, I'm sure he's on my side.

It was two crayons that played tic-tac-toe on the wall.
Fred and I had nothing to do with it at all.
I really think you should believe me—it's true,
That Y brought the yummy gum and the yellow yo-yo, too.

So if **Z** brings a zebra that leaves a great big mess,
Do not think for a minute that it is Fred and me in a dress.
Because yesterday I found an **A** and it brought **B** to **Z**,
And all the mess that you see here has **NOTHING** to do with me!